The Sun and the Mayfly

First published in Great Britain in 2022
by Little Steps Publishing
Vicarage House, 58-60 Kensington Church Street
London W8 4DB
www.littlestepspublishing.co.uk

ISBN: 978-1-912678-59-4

A CIP catalogue record for this book is available from the British Library.

Edited by Tasha Evans
Designed by Celeste Hulme
Printed in China
1 3 5 7 9 10 8 6 4 2

Little
Steps
PUBLISHING

The Sun and the Mayfly

Tang Tang

Illustrated by Zhang Xiao

Little Mayfly slowly flew
upwards from the lake, and
at the same time ...

... a bright yellow light rose up into the sky.
'Hello! You are amazing. You light up this world as
soon as you wake up,' called out Little Mayfly.

'Hello Little Mayfly,' said the Sun.
'Who are you?' uttered Little Mayfly.
'I'm the Sun.'

'I'm so happy to meet you! I only live
for one day. Are you the same as me?'
asked Little Mayfly.

The Sun didn't answer and gradually
rose higher into the sky.

Little Mayfly flapped her tiny wings, flying here and flying there, dancing around the beautiful wildlife and nature.

'I'm Little Mayfly. Who are you?'

'I'm Dragonfly.'

'I'm Little Mayfly. Who are you?'

'I'm Dog's Tail Grass.'

'I'm Little Mayfly. Who are you?'.

'I'm Dandelion.'

'I'm Little Mayfly. Who are you?'

'I'm Spider.'

After a while, Little Mayfly looked up and found that the Sun was much higher than before.

'Where are you going?' Little Mayfly asked.
'To the other side of the sky, and then the day is over,' the Sun replied.
'Oh, how lucky we are to have one whole day to live!' burst out Little Mayfly.

The Sun became quiet and didn't know what to say.

At that moment, a tadpole called out to Little Mayfly and said, 'Will you watch me shed my tail and grow four legs to become a frog?'

'I would love to,' answered Little Mayfly. 'I have one whole day to live.'

'One day? It takes me two months to become a frog, and then three years after that to become a big frog,' exclaimed the tadpole.

Plan ...

Swim for 10 hours every day

Eat 30 flies every day

2 months

3 months

Read books

Sing the Song of Frogs once every day

Goal

3 years

Travel around the world

'How long is that?' queried Little Mayfly.
'One month has many days and one year has
many, many more,' replied the tadpole.
'Oh well, I suppose I can't watch you become a
frog then,' said Little Mayfly disappointedly.

Before long, Little Mayfly met a duck who was hatching her eggs.
'My ducklings will be hatching soon,' quacked the duck.
'Wow! I will wait here for them to come out. I have one whole day
to live,' said Little Mayfly proudly.

'One day? But my ducklings won't be coming out for at
least 10 days,' the duck cried.
'Oh well, I can't watch your lovely ducklings come out
then,' said Little Mayfly.

Little Mayfly rested a moment on a flower bud.
'I'm an extremely beautiful flower. You will know it when I start to bloom,' announced the flower bud.
'Oh, how lovely! I will wait here for you to bloom then. I have one whole day to live,' said Little Mayfly.
'One day? But I won't bloom until tomorrow,' sighed the flower bud.
'What is tomorrow?' asked Little Mayfly.

'The day after today is tomorrow.
But you only have today, no
tomorrow,' the flower bud replied.

'Oh well, I can't watch you turn into a beautiful flower then,' sighed Little Mayfly.

Little Mayfly decided to rest a while.

Soon the Sun drifted over Little Mayfly's head.
'Are you upset?' asked the Sun.
'A little bit,' said Little Mayfly. 'We only have one day to live.
Are you not upset too?'

'Well, I've been living for a long, long time, and I will be living
for a long, long time too,' replied the Sun.

Little Mayfly didn't answer, she just flapped her tiny, pretty wings in the beaming sunlight.

'Sun, what's it like living beyond one day,' asked Little Mayfly.

The Sun thought for a moment before saying, 'The day passes into the night, and then the night passes into the day. That's it really.'

'I see, now I understand,' said Little Mayfly softly.

'Also spring passes into summer, summer passes into autumn, autumn passes into winter, winter passes into spring, spring passes into summer ...' explained the Sun.

'At the moment, it's summer.'

'Now I understand,'
whispered Little Mayfly.

'There are sunny days, rainy days,
windy days and snowy days ...
Today is a sunny day,' said the Sun.

'I understand. If only I could live for many days,' cried Little Mayfly.

After dozing for a while, Little Mayfly thought about what the Sun had said. 'But I do have a whole day,' she declared.

Then Little Mayfly flew from one grass to another and from one flower to another. She found that the higher she flew, the more of the world she could see.

'How big is the world?' Little Mayfly asked the Sun.
'The world is very big indeed. Beyond this lake, there are villages, fields, grasslands, forests, deserts, seas, rivers, mountains, cities and glaciers,' exclaimed the Sun.

Little Mayfly flew up towards
the tallest trees.
'Sun, are you going down now,'
asked Little Mayfly.

'That's right. When you can't see me,
then one day is over,' said the Sun,
worried that Little Mayfly would be
very upset.

But instead Little Mayfly flew higher and said, 'Thank you for telling me so many things, now I'm going to fly to you.'

'I'm far, far away, Little Mayfly,' shouted the Sun.
'I'm not afraid of the long distance,' called out Little Mayfly.
'You won't be able to make it. I'm really, really far away,' the
Sun said seriously.
'But I want to give it a try. The longer I fly, the closer I'll be
to you,' cried Little Mayfly.
'In that case, I'm waiting for you,' said the Sun.

As Little Mayfly flickered and flew with her tiny, shiny wings flapping as fast as they could, the Sun stopped and waited for her.

After some time, Little Mayfly couldn't fly anymore. She gathered up her wings and gently floated down to the lake.
At the same time, the Sun went down too.

Darkness came...

then it was time for the Sun to shine
once more, beaming brightly on the lake,
shining on every precious living thing.